MW00885723

Danny in the Toybox

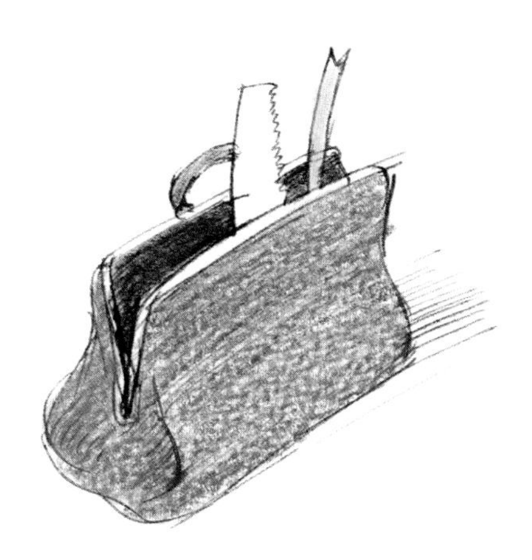

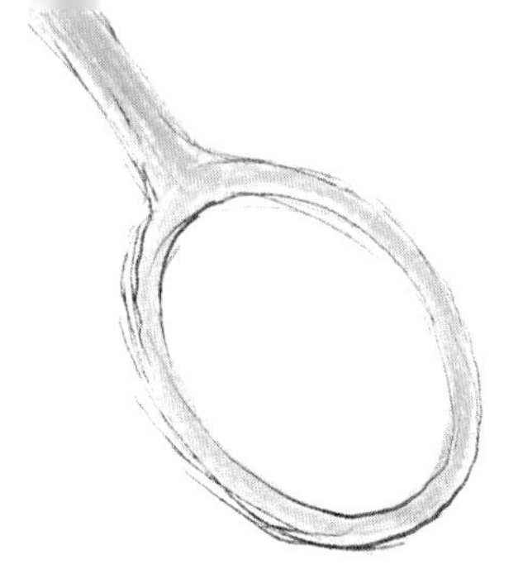

To Laura
R.T.

First published in 1990 in Australia by
Ashton Scholastic Pty. Limited
Printed in Hong Kong
The artwork for this book was executed in pen and ink
with watercolor pencil and colored pencils.
First U.S. edition, 1991
1 3 5 7 9 10 8 6 4 2

Library of Congress Cataloging in Publication Data
Tulloch, Richard. Danny in the toybox /
by Richard Tulloch; pictures by Armin Greder.
p. cm Summary: Danny is so cross that he climbs into his
toybox and declares that he is not coming out for the rest of his life.
ISBN 0-688-10501-7 (trade)—ISBN 0-688-10502-5 (lib.)
[1. Anger—Fiction.] I. Greder, Armin, ill. II. Title.
PZ7.T82315Dan 1991 [E]—dc20
90-24637 CIP AC

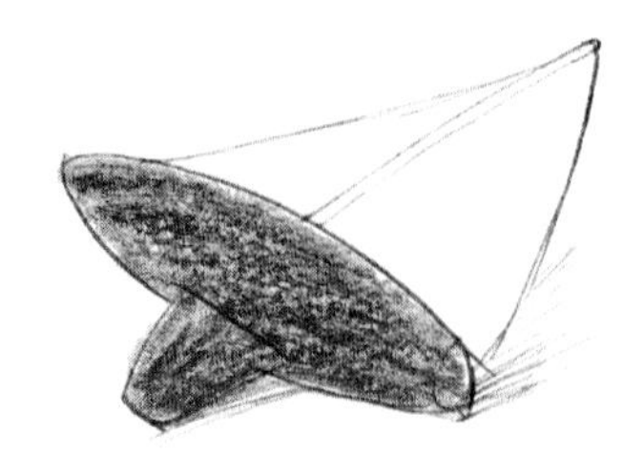

a story by Richard Tulloch

Danny · in the · Toybox

illustrated by Armin Greder

TAMBOURINE BOOKS
NEW YORK

Danny was mad.

He shouted and screamed at the top of his voice. He lay on the ground and pounded his fists and stomped his feet.

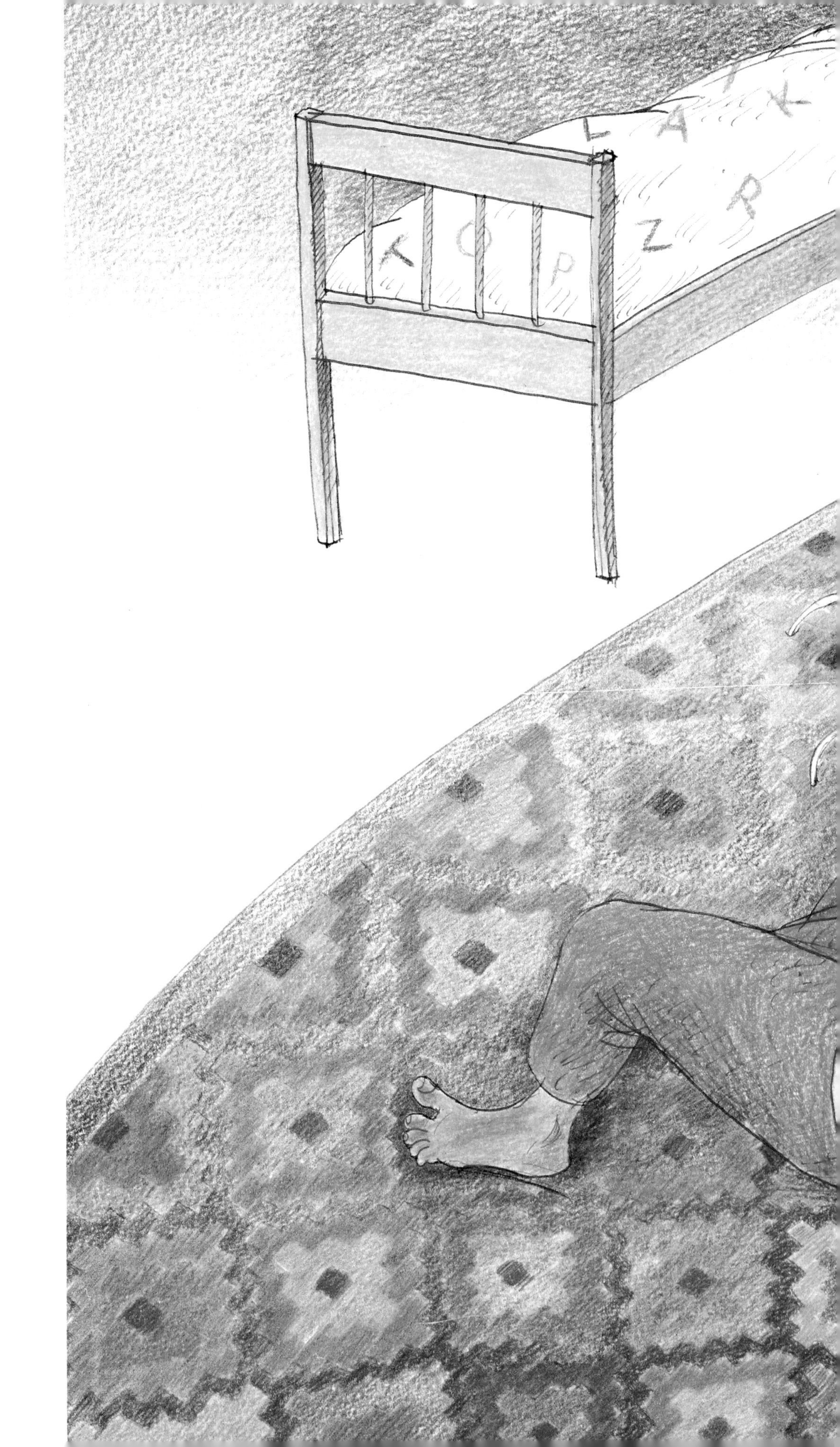

He threw his toys all over the floor. And he climbed into the toybox at the end of his bedroom and said, "I'm never coming out for the rest of my life. Never, never, never, so there!"

And he slammed the lid. Bang!

His little sister, Emma, tapped on the lid of the toybox. "Please come out, Danny. Please, please, pleeeeease! I neeeeed you to help me do my Funny Bunny jigsaw puzzle. Please, Danny, pleeeeease!"

But Danny said, "No!"

He opened the lid just a crack and hissed at Emma, "I'm never coming out for the rest of my life. Never, never, never, so there!"

Then he slammed the lid. Bang!

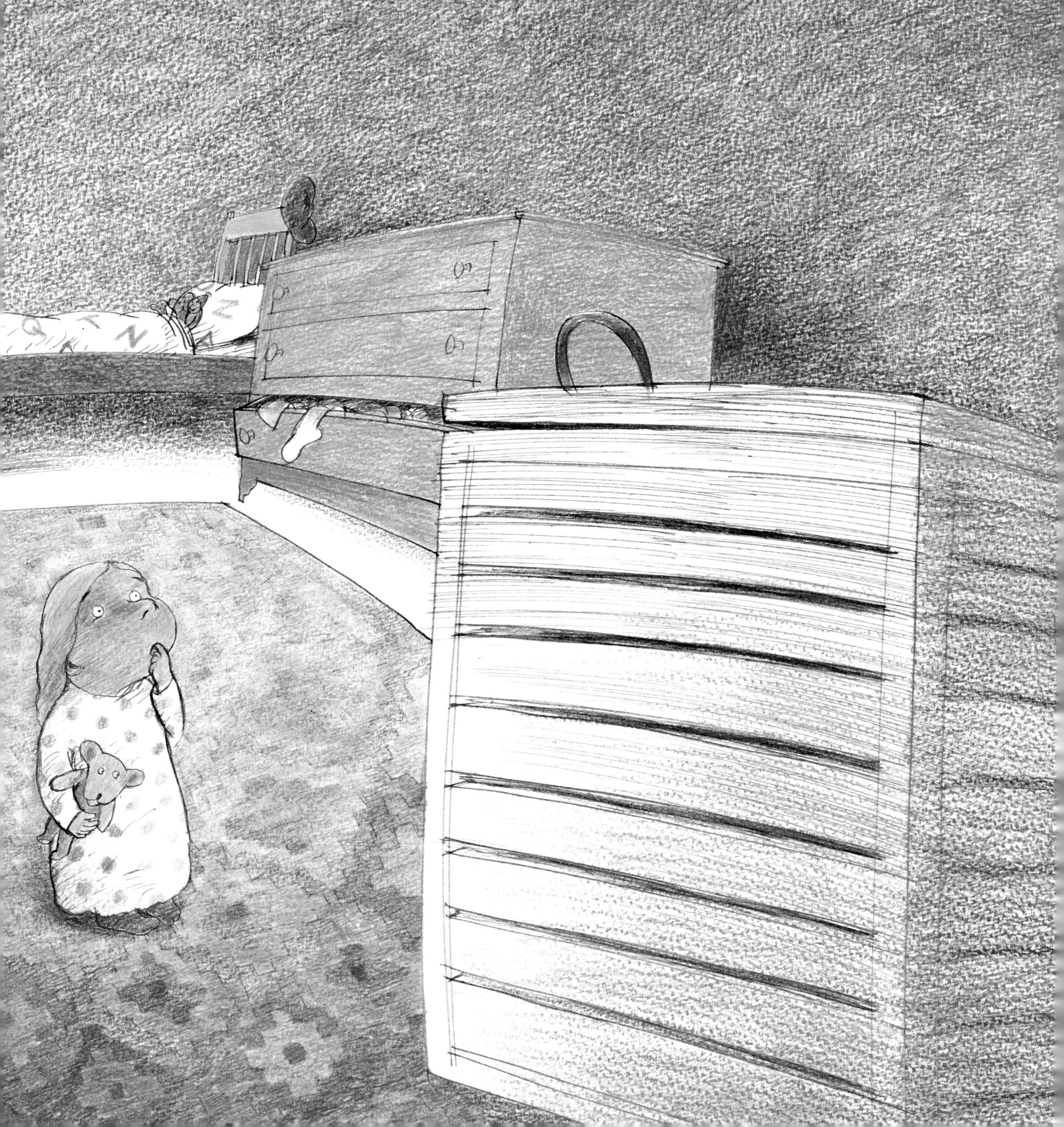

Danny's dog, Rumpus, scratched the lid of the toybox, whining and whimpering as if to say, "Come on out, Danny. Let's go for a walk and you can throw sticks for me to chase and I'll find some mud to roll in."

But Danny said, "No!"

He opened the lid of the toybox and growled at Rumpus in his deepest doggy voice, "I'm never coming out for the rest of my life. Never, never, never, so there!"

Then he slammed the lid. Bang!

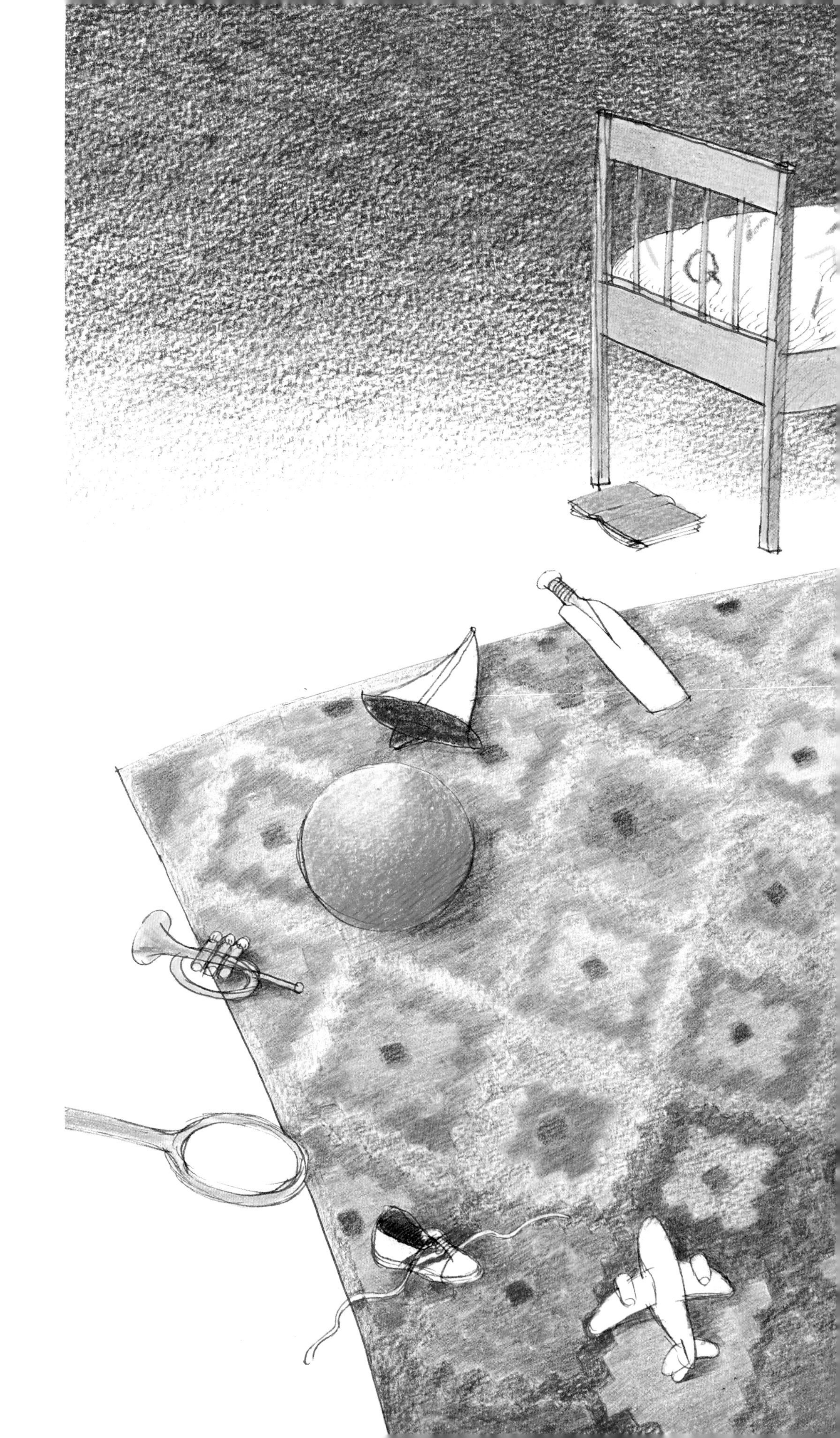

By now, Danny's mother was mad too. She banged on the lid of the toybox and said in a very stern voice, "I've had just about enough of your nonsense, Danny. If you don't come out by the time I count to three . . ."

But Danny said, "No!"

He opened the lid of the toybox and said to his mother in his firmest, strictest voice, "I'm never coming out for the rest of my life! Never, never, never, so there!"

Then he slammed the lid. Bang!

Danny's father sat down on the edge of the bed with one hand on his headache. He said, "Be reasonable, Danny. You'll have to come out sometime. And we're having Grandma's special treat for dessert—homemade apricot ice cream!"

But Danny said, "No!"

He opened the lid of the toybox, and told his father calmly and quietly, "I'm never coming out for the rest of my life. Never, never, never, so there!"

Then he slammed the lid. Bang!

A little while later a doctor arrived with a bag of doctor instruments.

She pressed her stethoscope against the side of the toybox and said in a wise doctor voice, "It isn't very healthy for a boy to live in a toybox, breathing stuffy air all day. And if Danny doesn't take a bath soon his feet will stink. He should come out now."

But Danny said, "No!"

He opened the lid of the toybox and explained into the end of the doctor's stethoscope, "I'm never coming out for the rest of my life! Never, never, never, so there!"

Then he slammed the lid. Bang!

The Fire Brigade arrived.

They ran through the house with their axes and their fire bell. The Little Firefighter stuck the end of the fire hose into Danny's toybox and called, "Can I turn the water on now?"

But the Fire Chief said, "Let me talk to him first."

"Listen here, young feller-me-lad," he said. "Suppose there was a fire. A boy stuck in a toybox would be a Serious Fire Hazard. So how about you come out now and we'll give you a ride in our fire truck?"

But Danny said, "No!"

He opened the lid of the toybox and made himself a megaphone with his hands and yelled at the Fire Chief at the top of his voice, "I'm never coming out for the rest of my life. Never, never, never, so there!"

Then he slammed the lid. Bang!

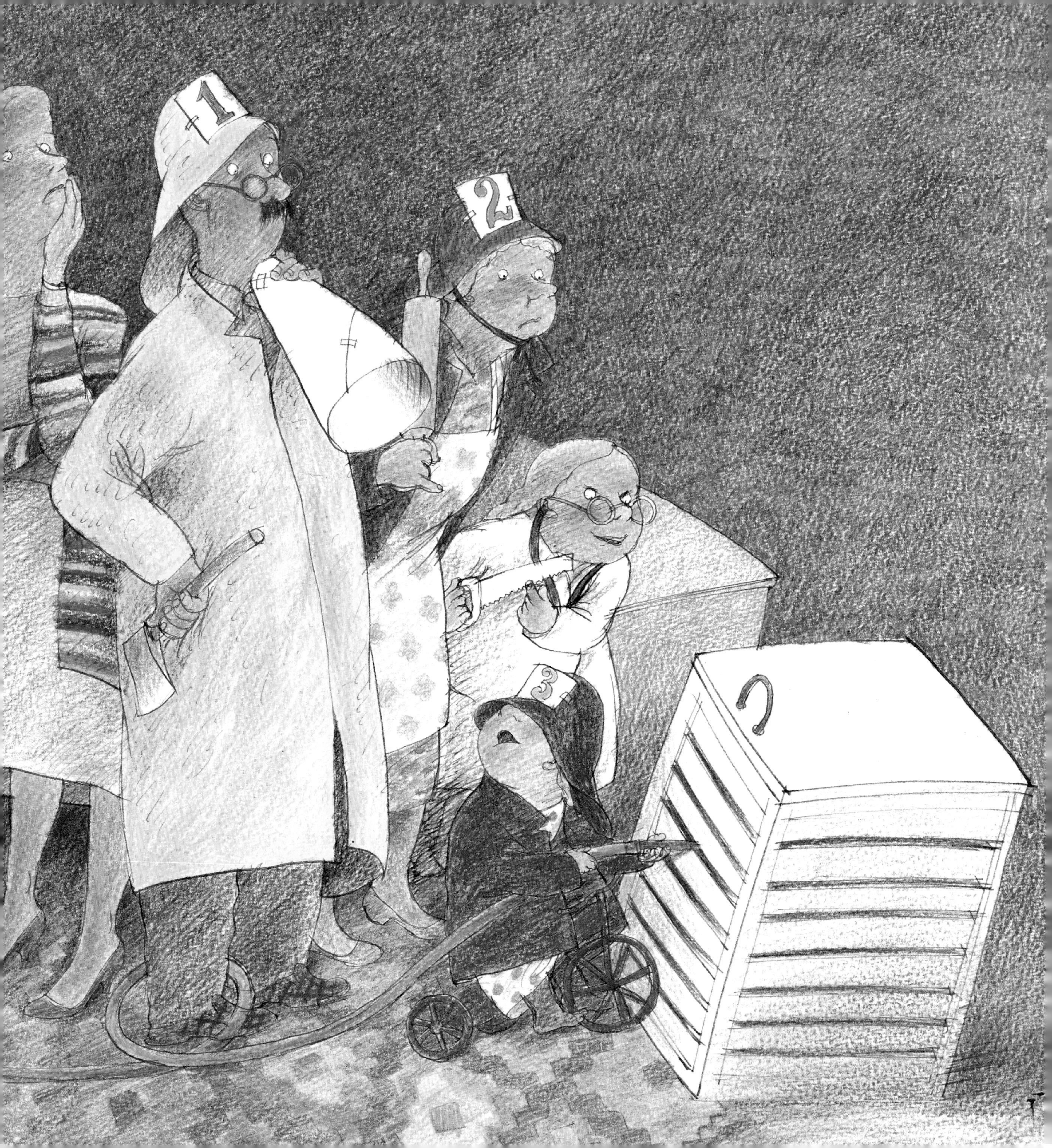
1
2
3

Then the Old Firefighter asked, "Why did Danny get into that toybox in the first place?"

"We don't know," said Danny's mother.

"He just gets mad sometimes," said Danny's father.

"One time when he was mad he took his pillow under our table and slept there all night," said the Little Firefighter.

2
1
3

"Well," said the Old Firefighter, "there isn't any law that says a person can't get mad. And there isn't any law that says a person can't sleep under a table or live in a toybox forever if they want to. Perhaps we should just leave Danny alone."

It was quiet in Danny's bedroom when everyone had gone.

Danny didn't care. He was mad. He was really very, very mad. He was really very, very, so extremely mad.

And it was all because . . .
It was all because . . .
It was because . . .

Danny couldn't remember
why he was really very, very,
so extremely mad.

So he stopped being mad
and climbed out of the
toybox . . .

and went off to eat some
homemade apricot ice cream.

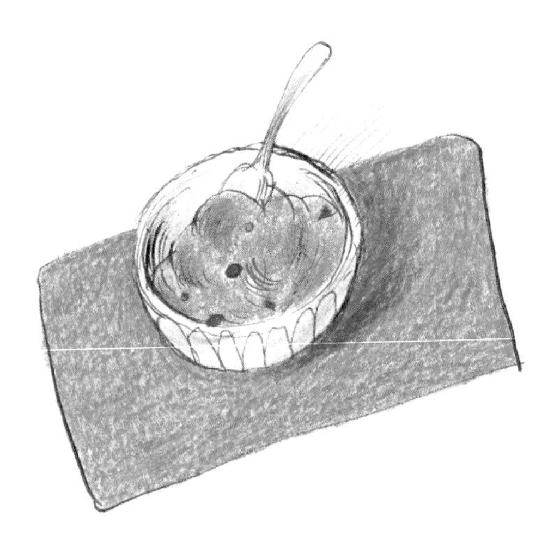